W9-DEC-890

FIC
DAN

Danko, Dan.

Operation squish!

$10.95

3930079151

DATE			

PRAIRIE VIEW MIDDLE SCHOOL
MEDIA CENTER
TINLEY PARK, IL 60477

BAKER & TAYLOR

Sidekicks

OPERATION SQUISH!

Sidekicks
OPERATION SQUISH!

by Dan Danko and Tom Mason

Illustrated by Barry Gott

PRAIRIE VIEW MIDDLE SCHOOL
MEDIA CENTER
TINLEY PARK, IL 60477

LITTLE, BROWN AND COMPANY
New York An AOL Time Warner Company

Copyright © 2003 by Dan Danko and Tom Mason
Illustrations copyright © 2003 by Barry Gott

All rights reserved. No part of this book may be reproduced in any form
or by any electronic or mechanical means, including information storage
and retrieval systems, without permission in writing from the publisher,
except by a reviewer who may quote brief passages in a review.

First Edition

The characters and events portrayed in this book are fictitious.
Any similarity to real persons, living or dead, is coincidental
and not intended by the author.

ISBN 0-316-16847-5 (hc)/ISBN 0-316-16846-7 (pb)
10   9   8   7   6   5   4   3   2   1
LAKE

Printed in the United States of America
The text for this book was set in Bookman,
and the display type is Bernhard Gothic Heavy Italic.

To Dave Sim —
thanks for the journey

Chapter One
Shhhh!

Ever had a secret? Like, I don't know, who you like at school or what is *really* under your bed. Yeah, I have those, too. But me, I have a secret so big you could fit all those other secrets inside it and still have room for all the eggheads in the school math club. My secret is so secret that I have to watch what I say and don't say, how I act, and most of all how fast I run.

Yeah, run. Why? Because I can run fast. Real fast. One hundred and two miles per hour. It used to be only 97 miles per hour, but lately, I've gotten better. Better at running, better at turning, and most important of all, better at stopping. (And if you don't think that's important, see how good *you* feel after you bounce off a mailbox at 48 miles per hour.)

But the biggest secret I have, the one I have to keep to myself no matter how much it kills me? Who I really am.

See, I'm thirteen and I've got a super power. When that happens, you can pretty much divide the world into three types of people: the good guys that want to arrest you; the bad guys that want to kill you; and people with no powers that just want you to appear on their talk shows.

I've decided to use my powers for good instead of evil, so luckily, no one wants to arrest me.

The bad guys just want to kill me.

Wait. Did I say *luckily?*

Anyway, that's why I have to keep my real identity a secret — to protect me and my family. It's all very complicated stuff. Just trust me when I say it makes life a whole lot easier when you just lie to all your friends and sneak around with a Spandex costume wadded up in your backpack.

Or at least as easy as life can be when an armor-wearing guy with a bad haircut, rotten teeth, and a silly plan to take over the world always seems to show up when you're out on a date.

Although I guess I'd have to be able to get a date in the first place before that can be a concern.

My secret identity is Guy Martin. That's the funny thing about having a super power. One day, the only secrets I had were some Web site links my parents didn't know about and my last report card that mysteriously "fell" into the flushing toilet before my dad could see it, and the next day everything about me was a secret. Suddenly, my real name, where I live, what I look like without big goggles and a midnight-blue Spandex uniform with a golden lightning bolt across the chest, where I go to school, all of it became totally hush-hush.

"Guard that information with your life, Speedy." That's what King Justice, founder of the League of Big Justice and the coolest superhero ever to wear Spandex, told me the day I was accepted into the League of Big Justice as a League of Big Justice Superhero Sidekick. "It's the burden of being a hero. Secrets! Danger! Creeping Spandex! Let no one! No one! Know! Your real! Identity! Or where you live! Not even Pumpkin Pete."

"Why? In case Pete's tortured and spills the beans?" I asked.

"No. Because he'll come over to your house and eat every last thing in your fridge. Trust me, I'm still finding Popsicle sticks behind my sofa."

I'm Pumpkin Pete's sidekick. Even though my power is super speed and my code name is Speedy, Pete likes to call me his "human bullet-proof vest."

"But I don't have the power to stop bullets," I told him the first time he called me that.

"You will if you're standing in front of me," he replied.

We didn't have a lot to talk about, Pete and I. Mostly Pete told me stories about his first days as a superhero and when he discovered he had "all the powers of a pumpkin."

"It was when I first used my pumpkin powers that I discovered I had all the powers of a pumpkin," he said.

"And what powers are those?" I asked.

"Pumpkin powers, kid. Pumpkin powers. All of 'em. Hand me my super-sized Big Gulp."

Pete only bought things with the word "super" in them because he thought it was a secret code for superheroes to know what products were the best. "Can you 'super-size' those fries for me?" he'll ask the employee at the drive-thru window. Pete'll hang his big fat orange head from the Pumpkinmobile and knowingly wink one large orange eye, as if to say, "See? I get it. I order 'super sizes' because I'm a 'superhero.'"

Pete also likes to hang out at supermarkets and thinks the Super Bowl is a top-secret toilet.

Chapter Two
Earlobe Lad Can't Fly

"Fly! Fly!" Pumpkin Pete shouted.

"Uh . . . Pete? He can't fly," I said and stepped next to him at the edge.

"Whaddaya mean he can't fly?" Pumpkin Pete snorted. "Look at those ears!"

"He has super hearing."

"No!" Pete gasped in disbelief and peered down from the roof. "You sure?"

I offered a silent nod.

"But the ears!" Pete stammered.

I shook my head.

"They're giant . . . They're the size of . . . He can just flap . . ."

"Super *hearing.*"

Earlobe Lad hit the ground with a dull thud that ended his panicked screaming and any doubts that he, in fact, could not fly. He rolled over on his back and let out a slight whimper, thankful nothing was broken.

"I'll be darned," Pumpkin Pete said. He scratched his wide orange chin and walked away from the edge of the Sidekick Super Clubhouse rooftop.

Chapter Three
Pumpkin Pete Trains the Sidekicks

"Okay!" Pumpkin Pete walked our line of sidekicks, staring down each one of us like an angry drill sergeant. "It's my turn to train you sidekicks! I'm going to teach you everything you need to know about being a superhero!"

He stopped and stared at Boom Boy.

"I can't fly!" Boom Boy shouted and prepared to run, fearful he'd be the next one thrown off the roof.

Boom Boy had a cool power: he could blow himself up. There was a small hitch, though. He didn't have the power to put himself back together, so he could do it only once, and then, well, bye-bye Boom Boy. He wore red and black

Spandex. On his chest was a picture of himself blowing up. Boom Boy was fourteen and liked to collect delicate crystal figurines.

"Don't worry, kid. I know you don't have the power to fly," Pumpkin Pete said, patting Boom Boy on the back. "But you *do* have the power to go make me a sandwich, don't you?"

Boom Boy nodded and raced toward the stairs, thankful to be out of harm's way — if only for a few minutes.

"And don't shaft me on the mayo!" Pumpkin Pete yelled after him.

Pete's fat orange pumpkin head rests atop his tall, narrow frame. Pigeons seem to follow him wherever he goes, awaiting the moment when his oversized gourd-head causes him to lose his balance one final time and he falls to the ground, splits open his bumpy pumpkin top, and spills hundreds of seeds across the sidewalk.

It's every pigeon's dream.

Pete's head *has* to be filled with seeds. Not because the pigeons eye him with such longing, but because heaven knows no brains will ever fall out of Pumpkin Pete's hollow orange skull.

"You think being a sidekick is *so* glamorous, don't you?" Pete shouted, spinning on his heel. "Sure, it would be *swell* if you only had to do my laundry, wash my Pumpkinmobile and clean the mold that grows between my pumpkin toes. Well I'm here to tell you being a sidekick is more than just fun! It's hard work! In fact, it's work that's so hard, you'll think, 'Wow! That hard work was really . . . really . . . uh . . . really . . . uh . . .'"

"Hard?" Spelling Beatrice offered.

Spelling Beatrice wears bright yellow colors and double-thick glasses that make her look like she has two small moons for eyes. Beatrice is seventeen. She's been a sidekick for almost three years and uses her uncanny spelling and grammar skills to fight crime.

"You bet it will be, Smelling Beatrice!" Pete confirmed.

"That's *Spelling* Beatrice," she corrected.

"Spelling?" Pumpkin Pete rolled his eyes. "Hey, I'm not here to tell you how to pick good names. I'm just here to teach you how to be superheroes. Now tell me, what's the most important thing every superhero must have?"

"Matching boots!" Spice Girl called out.

Exact Change Kid raised his hand and shook it violently in the air.

"Yes, Quarter Man?" Pumpkin Pete said.

"Shouldn't we wait until Earlobe Lad and Boom Boy come back?" Exact Change Kid asked.

Pumpkin Pete leaned over the edge of the Sidekick Super Clubhouse rooftop. "Hey! Ear Boy. What's the most important thing every super-hero must have?"

"I think . . . my spleen is ruptured," Earlobe Lad groaned from the grass below.

Pete turned back to face the rest of us. "He said 'a spleen.' He's wrong."

"Is it courage?" Exact Change Kid offered.

"Courage!? Yeah. Right," Pumpkin Pete chuckled. "No, the correct answer is . . . insurance!"

"Ohhh. Of course. Insurance," Spice Girl said in a slow voice, shaking her head. Spice Girl had short blond hair. Her outfit was entirely pink with a purple "Girl Power" patch stuck on the front. If brains were the only thing that made you a superhero, Spice Girl would definitely be a villain.

"If the bad guys don't kill you, the lawsuits will, let me tell you! I still can't go back to the state of New Jersey." He paused for a moment as an old memory flashed into his head. "Stupid blue wire," Pumpkin Pete grumbled in a low voice.

I-N-S-U-R-A-N-C-E, Exact Change Kid carefully spelled out in his thick notebook. He had a crew cut, was thin, wore thin goggles that doubled as eyeglasses, and was decked out in white Spandex with red boots. When he wasn't fighting crime, which was pretty much every minute of the day, Exact Change Kid liked to categorize his lint collection by cotton density.

"What's the second most important thing a superhero can have?" Pumpkin Pete questioned.

"More insurance!" Spice Girl enthused.

"Mmmpa mam pam!" Boy-in-the-Plastic-Bubble Boy said, his thick Hamster Ball of Justice muffling his every word. What does Boy-in-the-Plastic-Bubble Boy look like? Hey, the name says all.

"Courage!" Exact Change Kid called out.

Pete stopped pacing in front of Exact Change Kid. "Someone hit you with a Kryptonite rock or something when you were a baby?"

Exact Change Kid silently shook his head "no."

"An agent," Pumpkin Pete finally informed us. "If you want to see real evil, try reading a corporate endorsement contract." Pete leaned back over the building's edge again. "You get that, Ear Kid? An *agent*."

There was silence.

"Ear Kid? Ear Kid?" Pumpkin Pete repeated.

"Got . . . it . . ." Earlobe Lad's weak, disembodied voice was barely loud enough to be heard.

"Do you think someone should help him?" I asked Spice Girl.

"I don't think so," she replied. "'An agent' isn't that hard to remember."

"If you want a sweet product-endorsement deal, you gotta have an agent." Pete reached into his Super Pumpkin Utility Bag. "And speaking of sweet, there's nothing sweeter and more refreshing than a cold Pow Soda." Pete popped open a can of Pow and took a big gulp. "End the crime spree of thirst with Pow Soda: The Soft Drink of Superheroes."

Exact Change Kid carefully wrote the second most important thing a superhero should have. *#2: Agent (e.g., Pow Soda [end/crime spree/ thirst]),* he neatly printed.

"We've got insurance. We've got an agent. Anyone want to guess the final thing every superhero must have?"

"An insurance agent!" Spice Girl gleefully chirped.

Exact Change Kid raised his pencil. Pete stabbed a long viney finger toward his face.

"Don't even think about it," Pumpkin Pete growled.

Exact Change Kid slowly lowered his pencil. *#3: NOT courage,* he wrote.

"A tailor," Pumpkin Pete said. "Let me tell you, when this Spandex starts to go bad . . . whew! Now there's a *real* crime."

Pete stopped pacing for a moment and finished off the final gulp of his Pow Soda. "Ahh. Refreshing to the last drop. Pow: The Soft Drink of Superheroes." Pete stopped for a moment and thought. "Okay," he began again, "class dismissed."

"Mamm pam pam mam mam! Mam mam pam!" Boy-in-the Plastic-Bubble Boy yelled. He rolled toward the stairs and past Boom Boy, who was finally returning with Pete's sandwich.

"Wait!" I yelled.

The sidekicks froze in their tracks. Or in Boy-in-the-Plastic-Bubble Boy's case, in his plastic bubble.

"Wait, wait, wait, wait." I didn't often repeat myself, but the words just came out, mostly because I was so surprised I had said them in the first place. Something just didn't feel right. We are sidekicks, teammates-in-training to the greatest superheroes on Earth.

King Justice. Lady Bug. Captain Haggis. The Stain. Mr. Ironic. The Good Egg. Ms. Mime. Depression Dave. The Librarian. Pumpkin Pete. These are the members of the League of Big

Justice. These are the greatest superheroes on Earth, and we sidekicks aspire to walk in their mighty shoes.

And *this* was the best training we could get?

"This isn't right," I said, searching for the words to express how I felt. "I . . . I want to help people, to make a difference. I didn't become a sidekick to be a pitchman for sodas and potato chips. There are people out there, people who don't have a voice, or who . . . who aren't strong enough to stand on their own. I want to be their voice. I want to be their strength! That's what every hero needs! Honor. Truth. Justice. And yes, courage! Not endorsements and tailors! We have to fight for those who cannot fight for themselves! It's about making this world a better place . . . not just for me, but for everyone! That's what a hero — no — that's what a *super*hero is!"

Pumpkin Pete looked up from his plate. He gripped Boom Boy's sandwich in one hand and another can of Pow Soda in the other. One cheek was packed with turkey and mayonnaise.

"Huh? Were you talking to me?" he asked.

Chapter Four
Dear Prudence

The next day at school, my best friend Miles and I sat in the corner of the cafeteria. I have side-kick duty every day after school and a full day on Saturday. The rest of the time, my life is pretty much normal, or as normal as it could be if you run around in Spandex with a guy who has a pumpkin for a head.

Jerry Stone shuffled up with his tray of spaghetti and meatballs. His glasses slid down to the tip of his greasy nose, and he made a rhythmic squeaking noise like a dog's chew toy with every step he took.

"Can I sit here?" he asked, pointing to the empty seat across from me.

"No. It's taken," I replied.

"By whom?"

"Prudence," Miles responded, knowing full well that I would not.

"Cane?" Jerry asked.

"Do you know another Prudence?" Miles snorted and bit into his baloney sandwich.

"But she's over there, having lunch with Mandrake Steel."

"Where?" I said, pretending not to know already.

"In the middle of all the other girls sitting with Mandrake. You can just see the top of her head when that brunette girl leans left. There!" Jerry pointed with his chin, both hands still securely fastened to the sides of his lunch tray.

It was easy to find Prudence in any crowd. She was the most popular girl at school. She was awesome. She was awesome like a beautiful, blond, black hole in the center of my universe sucking everything toward her. Except, well, she didn't have infinite density and she was only thirteen.

"Yeah, well . . . she asked me to save her seat until she came back," I added.

Jerry looked down at his spaghetti, then

looked toward Prudence Cane. He looked back at the empty seat, then once more to Prudence and finally locked both eyes on his meatball.

"Just like yesterday?" Jerry whined.

"Yes. Just like yesterday," I grumbled.

Mandrake said something and all the girls surrounding him giggled in unison. Jerry shuffled away, staring down onto the lone meatball on his tray, his rhythmic squeaks dying away beneath the laughter of Prudence Cane.

"Why do you do that every day?" Miles asked.

"Every day? That's only the fifteenth time I told Jerry he couldn't sit with us," I defended.

"This month," Miles added. "But why do you save a seat for Prudence every day? I mean, do you really think she'll come over here and sit next to you?"

"I can't believe you're asking me that, Miles!" I spat back. "Imagine, okay, imagine that one day Prudence comes into the cafeteria and all the seats are already taken. What happens if *that's* the day I didn't save her a seat? What happens *then*, Miles?"

"Uh . . . she eats outside on the quad?"

"Exactly! Outside where . . . well . . . where who knows what might happen to her! I'm not doing this for me. The seat-saving — defending this lone sitting place from the Jerry Stones of the world — it's not for me, I tell you. I'm doing it for Prudence. My promise to protect the innocent doesn't end when I take off the mask, Miles."

"You made a promise to protect the innocent?" Miles asked.

"Well, not really the innocent. Just Pumpkin Pete. He made me promise."

"Protect him against what?"

"Bunny rabbits. He hates bunny rabbits."

"Promise me, kid! Promise me you'll never let those furry balls of evil get to me!" Pumpkin Pete had said to me, both hands gripping my shoulders.

"I promise . . ."

"They . . . they . . . they don't think I know," he'd gasped, his chest heaving. "But I do. I know all about their malicious, cuddly plan of doom."

"What plan of doom?" I had wanted to know.

"The cuddly one, my little Human Bulletproof Vest. The cuddly one."

"Pete, I really can't stop bullets," I had reminded him.

"Don't start that again, kid," Pete had huffed.

*   *   *

"Wow," Miles said, biting another mouthful of baloney. "I always knew those bunnies were up to something."

"Easter is a real difficult time for Pete."

Miles is the only kid in school who knows I'm secretly a sidekick. And just like the other kids in school, Prudence doesn't know Mandrake is also Charisma Kid and sidekick to King Justice. Charisma Kid has all the power and confidence of a really great smile. That kind of ability just doesn't disappear when you take off a costume.

Just ask Prudence.

I drummed my fingers on the table. "There must be some way I can get Prudence to notice me."

Notice me instead of Mandrake Steel? Yeah. Right. Even his name is better than mine. Mandrake *Steel*. Steel. Strong. Shiny. Unbreakable. And Guy *Martin*. I looked up "Martin" in the dictionary. It said, "A bird of the swallow genus with a notched or square tail." Like *that's* going to win Prudence Cane over from a guy who's so good-looking and popular, he was elected homecoming king *and* queen.

"Why don't you coincidentally bump into her in your Speedy costume?" Miles offered. "She'd probably go for the sidekick thing."

"That is so pathetic. Do you really think I'm such a loser that I'd use my powers and position as a sidekick to get a date with Prudence? My sidekick vows are precious to me! It would be a total mockery of everything I believe and . . . and . . . everything the League of Big Justice stands for. I'm a superhero sidekick, Miles! And that means more to me than any date with Prudence Cane! It means honor, truth, justice, and, yes, courage!"

I turned my back on Miles and gritted my teeth.

Prudence and Mandrake left the cafeteria together. Mandrake took a moment to look back over his shoulder and throw me a victorious wink.

The large sign hung above my head in big green letters. Miles and I sat behind a table on the school quad. At least two dozen students, mostly girls, stood in a line that serpentined around the corner. The girl at the head of the group finished writing her name on a blank piece of paper. She folded it in half and dropped it into a huge box in front of me.

"Is it going to be a real sidekick!?" the girl gushed.

"Just like the sign says." I nodded. "Just like the sign says."

WIN A DATE WITH A LEAGUE OF BIG JUSTICE SUPER-HERO SIDEKICK! the green letters screamed.

"I hope it's Charisma Kid," the girl said with a sigh and ran off to class.

So much for honor, truth, justice, and, yes, courage.

Chapter Five
Honor, Truth, Justice, and Blah Blah Blah

The next day at the Sidekick Super Clubhouse, Charisma Kid slapped me on the back while I sat in front of the Sidekick Super Computer. "I heard about that lame stunt you pulled at school the other day."

"It's nothing," I said.

"Yeah. Nothing," Charisma Kid replied. "That is, if you consider winning a date with a *real* sidekick 'nothing.'"

The only thing that could have made this worse was if the other sidekicks were there to hear.

"What? Did someone say I could win a date with a real sidekick?" Earlobe Lad asked, sticking his head in from the other room as if he was reading my mind and wished to deepen my humiliation. "Is it Spice Girl?"

"No!" I huffed. "It's not Spice Girl!"

"Who is it, then?" Earlobe Lad asked.

I paused and looked at the ground.

"I don't know."

"You don't know? If it's not Spice Girl, I sure don't want to win."

"Then don't enter the contest," I grumbled.

"If I did win, could I choose Spice Girl?" Earlobe Lad wondered. "Or do I have to go on the date with whomever you choose?"

"I . . . I don't know. I really haven't thought about the rules."

"Rules to what?" Boom Boy asked, wandering into the room.

"Speedy's got a contest where you can win a date with a Sidekick!" Earlobe Lad whispered.

"Is it Spice Girl!? No way!" Boom Boy gushed. "Hey. Hey. How come no one told me?"

I shrugged.

"That's who I'm picking if I win," Earlobe Lad quietly informed the room.

"Oh, I see how it is," Boom Boy began. "Don't tell Boom Boy so he doesn't have a chance to win a date with Spice Girl. So that's how it's going to be, is it?"

"But we're telling you now, Boom Boy," Earlobe Lad whispered.

"'Cause you knew if you didn't . . . if you didn't . . . I swear, I'll blow myself up!"

"Go ahead!" Earlobe Lad challenged.

"What's going on?" Exact Change Kid walked into the room with a fistful of rolled quarters.

"Boom Boy's threatening to blow himself up." I watched his face turn a deeper shade of red. "Again."

"What!? And nobody called me!?"

"I didn't think you'd be interested. I mean, it doesn't seem like your kinda thing." In fact, I was surprised Exact Change Kid had an interest in anything that didn't involve disinfectant, spread-sheets, or coins.

"Well," he sheepishly began, "I *am* a bit curious to see if he can really blow up. And usually, he doesn't threaten to blow himself up until *at least* three o'clock." He scanned the acoustic tile ceiling. "Although cleanup will be a real pain."

Boom Boy's eyes bulged slightly and his whole head shook.

"Hey, guys." Spelling Beatrice walked into the

room and plopped in front of the Sidekick Super Computer.

"Hel-lo!" Boom Boy grunted the two syllables through teeth gritted tighter than a fresh set of orthodontist's braces.

"Is it three o'clock already?" Spelling Beatrice tapped the watch on her wrist. "My watch must be slow."

"No, he's ahead of schedule today," Exact Change Kid explained.

"Wow. What happened?" she asked.

"Speedy's having a contest to win a date with Spice Girl," Earlobe Lad complained. "And he didn't include Boom Boy."

"Gnnt! Hrr! Grrrrnnng!" In response to Earlobe Lad's comment, Boom Boy doubled over as if someone had just punched him in the gut. He tightened his stomach muscles and clenched his teeth even tighter.

"What!?" Exact Change Kid burst out. "I can win a date with Spice Girl!? Why didn't anyone tell me!?"

"Because there *is* no contest to win a date with Spice Girl!" I protested.

"Ohhhh! You won't trick me like you did Boom Boy," Exact Change Kid warned. "Sure, you'll eliminate one member of the competition once Boom Boy explodes, but I'm on to you!"

"Wait!" Boom Boy said. He opened his eyes and stood up. "I get it now. I get it. You *want* me to blow up, don't you? Yeah. 'Cause once I do, I'll be gone and then there'll be no more Boom Boy to win a date with Spice Girl."

"THERE IS NO CONTEST TO WIN A DATE WITH SPICE GIRL!" I yelled.

"Ahhh!" Earlobe Lad screamed and grabbed his oversized ears, unable to control the sensitivity of his super hearing. He fell to the ground and flopped around like a landed fish. "Doesn't anybody know how to whisper!?"

"Tell them who they really *can* win a date with, Spuddo." Charisma Kid chuckled.

For a brief moment, the confusion stopped. Earlobe Lad, Exact Change Kid, and Boom Boy all stared at me. Well, Earlobe Lad didn't stare exactly. He just stopped squirming and peered up at me from the Clubhouse corner.

"Well?" Exact Change Kid asked.

I hung my head and mumbled, "Me."

"What?" The word burst from Exact Change Kid's mouth.

"Me," I mumbled again.

"He said, 'Me,'" Charisma Kid informed them with a grin.

"I can win a date with you?" Spelling Beatrice perked up at the Sidekick Super Computer and spun around in her chair to face Charisma Kid.

"Hmmm," Boom Boy thought for a moment. "I'll still enter."

"No, not *me*. Him." Charisma Kid pointed at me.

"Speedy!?" Boom Boy shouted. "I almost blew myself up over Speedy!?"

"Why do all of you hate me so?" Earlobe Lad cried out at Boom Boy's booming voice. He ran from the room, fleeing the sense-shattering sounds of normal human conversation.

"Look, it's a contest at my school, okay?" I did my best to control my anger. I didn't want Charisma Kid to know he was getting to me. "One of the students will get to win a date with me. That's all."

"What if we want to win a date with Spice Girl?" Boom Boy asked.

"If you want to go out with her so bad, just ask her out already!" I was cracking under the frustration.

Boom Boy and Exact Change Kid looked at each other and rolled their eyes.

"And risk rejection?" Exact Change Kid said with a laugh.

"I'd rather win her over through something deceitful like a contest, then give her the chance to get to know the real me," Boom Boy stated.

I shook my head. "Sorry. It's not Spice Girl. Not Charisma Kid. Just me."

"And that's how it better stay, because if I find out it *is* Spice Girl . . . I swear, I swear I'll blow myself up!" Boom Boy threatened.

I looked at the ground and wished I could be anyplace else. "Yeah."

"Although, I will say, you must be pretty desperate," Boom Boy laughed.

"I'm not desperate! I'm . . . I'm . . ."

"Desperate." Boom Boy patted me on the back and left the room.

"Hey, I already know *I'm* desperate!" Exact Change Kid chimed in. "Mind if I steal your idea? 'Win a Date with Exact Change Kid!' And I thought *I* was the brains of this outfit!"

And the saddest thing? He is.

Exact Change Kid whipped open his notebook and began plotting his own contest, wandering off into the Sidekick Super Kitchen of Justice and Food.

Spice Girl passed him in the doorway and

skipped into the Monitor Room of Waitingness. "What'd I miss?"

"Everyone's mad at Speedy because they thought he was having a contest to win a date with Spice Girl," Spelling Beatrice explained.

"Win a date with Spice Girl!" Spice Girl cheered. "I want to win a date with Spice Girl!"

"I heard that!" Boom Boy shouted from the other room.

Spice Girl grabbed a pencil and awaited instructions. I stared at her in silence and saw the dim light bulb of realization slowly brighten above her head.

"Oh, wait . . . *I'm* Spice Girl." She looked at the pencil in her hand as her smile slowly faded. "I probably can't even enter. I'm sad now."

"Whatever." I just wanted to leave. The funny thing was, this whole date contest seemed like such a killer idea when Prudence Cane was standing in line with all the other girls at my school.

"If I win, can I choose Charisma Kid instead?" Spice Girl wondered.

"If you win, you can choose anyone you want." I sighed.

"*ANYONE!?* I'm blowing myself up! I swear!" Boom Boy shouted from the other room.

Spice Girl clapped her hands and raced from the room like a cheerleader running toward the quarterback after the winning touchdown.

A laugh exploded from Charisma Kid's mouth. He stopped for a moment and sucked in a lungful of air, then continued laughing until a single tear rolled down his cheek.

"So . . . what're you going to do to make sure Prudence is the winner?" he asked, finally calming enough to speak.

"What makes you think I care if she wins?"

"Because every time she's around, I'd swear your super power was drooling. Or is staring like an idiot watching a puppet show a side effect of super speed?"

I didn't respond. I pulled up a chair next to Spelling Beatrice. "Want to play Scrabble?"

Wow. That's how desperate I was. I actually asked a human dictionary to play Scrabble.

"I know what you're going to do," Charisma Kid continued, leaning next to me on the Sidekick Super Computer. "You're going to throw out all the other girls' entries and stuff the box with Prudence Cane's name, aren't you?"

I spun around in my chair like an exploding top.

"You are so STUPID!" I yelled, finally losing

control. "It's just a stupid contest and I don't care who wins and your ideas are stupid and there is no way I'm stuffing the stupid box with Prudence Cane's stupid name! So why don't you go smile at a stupid bank robber or something!"

The Spandex tightened across my chest with each deep breath I took to calm down. Charisma Kid looked at me, almost as if he had taken my yelling as a challenge.

"Loser," he sneered and left the room.

I spun my chair back around to face the Sidekick Super Computer. Spelling Beatrice rubbed my shoulder to show her support.

"You've told me how much you like Prudence," she said softly after a moment of silence. "How *are* you going to be sure she wins?"

I slammed my fist against the tabletop.

"I'm stuffing the stupid box with her stupid name, okay!?"

Chapter Six
A Visit with the King

I wandered out of the Sidekick Super Clubhouse and across the League of Big Justice Super Two-Hours-Free Parking Lot for Visitors with Parking Validation of Justice, under the League of Big Justice Super Justice Arch and through the League of Big Justice Super Justice Revolving Door. The League of Big Justice Super Justice Lobby was empty.

I walked down the Hall of Heroes of Big Justice and stopped at the League of Big Justice Super Souvenir Gift Shop.

Dozens of twelve-inch Pumpkin Pete action figures stood on racks outside the shop. NOW WITH REAL PUMPKIN ACTION™! the sign read. In much smaller print beneath, it stated: PUMPKIN ACTION™ SOLD SEPARATELY. I pulled a Pete figure from the shelf and pressed its chest.

"I have all the powers of a pumpkin!" it proudly boasted in a tiny robotic voice. "Buy me more accessories!" the voice chimed as I placed it back on the shelf.

"Pumpkin Pete wanted them to say 'Death to all bunnies!' but Wal-Mart refused to carry such anti-bunny products. A conspiracy? Perhaps. Perhaps. Only the bunnies know for certain."

I turned to face King Justice. He had been watching me. I don't know for how long or where he came from, but he was there now. King Justice was so big, a small family could live in his shadow. A red, white, and blue shield was plastered across his chest like a giant billboard of patriotic graffiti.

"There's something I . . . I was just wondering . . ."

"Speak, and let my wise words mold you like the shapeless ball of sticky goo that you are." King Justice walked across the Super Carpet of Big Shag to join me at the souvenir shop.

I paused for a moment, unsure I should even ask. "Do you have insurance?" I finally said.

"Insurance!?"

"I know! I'm sorry! It's a stupid question!"

"I dare say you've shattered the cosmic boundaries of the absurd!" King Justice agreed, and gave a quick laugh under his breath.

I couldn't remember the last time I felt this embarrassed. Oh, wait. Yes, I could. It was five minutes ago when I had to admit my contest was to win a date with me.

"Do I have insurance? Of all the —" King Justice looked me in the eye. "Of course I have insurance! If the bad guys don't kill you, the lawsuits will, let me tell you! Pumpkin Pete still can't go back to the state of New Jersey." He paused for a moment, as an old memory flashed into his head. "I *told* him the red wire," he grumbled in a low voice.

King Justice's admission hit me harder than if he had used his own Five Knuckles of Justice to belt me in the head. I didn't want to ask the next question, but I had to.

"I suppose you have an agent, too?"

"Better an agent to drink the bitter wine of the lawyer's grape than King Justice, chum. If you want to see real evil, try reading a corporate endorsement contract."

I felt my enthusiasm for life leak out of me faster than hot air in an overblown balloon with a nail hole. This was King Justice, my idol, the world's idol, and to him being a superhero was just about having a good agent, insurance, and probably even a —

"Now allow me to wrap you in the soft, quilty blanket of inquiry," King Justice began. I didn't look up. I didn't have the energy and I was afraid of what he was about to say. "Have you plucked a tailor from the ranks of many? Being a new sidekick, the thought of you stuck with someone second-rate just makes me want to puke. When this Spandex starts to go bad . . . whew! Now there's a *real* crime."

"I've got to go home, now," I mumbled. "I don't think you need my help anymore. You seem to have all you need."

"All I need? Agents and tailors and insurance are important, my young pup, but there's more to being a superhero than that."

"Oh, sure. Sure," I mumbled. "It's also about using your powers to get a date with a girl who doesn't know you exist. And I'm sure a movie deal. And having your own action figure — a limited-edition, collector's-item action figure with kung-fu grip and super-action punch."

"WHAT ARE YOU SAYING, BOY!?" King Justice burst from the bench. "Your action figure has kung-fu grip *and* super-action punch!? They told me it couldn't be done!"

"No. No. I don't have an action figure. I don't . . . I don't think I want one anymore. Good-bye, King. Good-bye."

I gave a long, last look at all the merchandise.

The Stain's Stain Remover.

Ms. Mime's Low-Fat Grill.

The Good Egg's Crime Fighting for Dummies.

Captain Haggis's Big Bag o' Haggis and Corn.

Depression Dave's *12 Steps to a Better You** *(*Results may vary).*

Mr. Ironic's Big Book of Coincidences.

King Justice's 50 Favorite Recipes. "I don't just fight crime . . ." the cover photo of King Justice blurted, "I fight *calories,* too!"

Yes, these were the members of the League of Big Justice. They fought villains. They battled tyrants. They punched evil in the face.

And it was all to make a buck.

"Did you know, just this lone shop made more than twelve million dollars last year," King Justice said, admiring his own cookbook.

"You must be proud." I tried to not be sarcastic. I *tried.*

"As proud as a beaver after a full day of log chewing. You can do a lot of things with that kind of money," King Justice said so matter-of-factly it actually shocked me. "A lot of things."

"I bet."

"Of course, most of it went to rebuild the library that was destroyed by the awesome numeric madness of the Dewey Decimator! But! There was still enough left in the coffers of good to repair the nearby homes that were damaged." King Justice picked up his cookbook and flipped through the pages. "Ohh! Seared ahi encrusted with sesame seeds in a miso-jalapeño sauce. One! Of! My! FAVORITES!"

"You mean . . . this shop . . . the money goes to charity?" Sure it was an obvious answer, but it didn't hurt to clarify sometimes.

"You didn't think we *kept* it, did you?" King Justice chuckled.

"*You!?* Keep the money for yourself!? *Pffft!* Noooooo! I'd never think that!" If I told a lie any bigger, my nose would've grown. "But why doesn't it say that anywhere?"

"Good doesn't need to pat itself on the back, lad."

Ouch.

"Even Pete's stuff goes to your charity?" I asked.

"No. That money goes to The Charity to Help Persons with Pumpkin Heads."

"But Pete is the only person in the world with a pumpkin head," I pointed out.

"I've always wondered about that." King Justice put his hand on my shoulder and led me outside. "Agents and insurance are important to being a hero, but they're not what makes a hero great."

"What is it, then?" I matched his pace, my super speed helping me keep up with King Justice's enormous strides.

The King stopped. He turned and placed both his hands on my shoulders and looked me square in the eyes.

"That is a road map you'll just have to read on your own, lad. Now if you'll excuse me, I must focus my keen Senses of Justice and muster every last ounce of my Kingness, for I believe I'm about to be crushed by that giant robot."

"Grrk gaaak guugle gort!" King Justice yelled from under the massive metallic heel of the giant robot.

"What?" I yelled back.

"Grrk gaak guugle gort!"

"Gort? What's a 'gort'?" I asked, trying not to panic.

"GORT! GORT!" he yelled more urgently from under the robot's foot.

It was like having Boy-in-the-Plastic-Bubble Boy read you a movie review.

The robot towered over the League of Big Justice. It must've been at least eighty feet tall. It had come from the sky, as silent as a cloud, and landed directly atop King Justice. He was practically invulnerable, but that just had to hurt.

I mean, he *was* eating cement under the foot of a giant robot and all.

The robot was steel blue with big, red, glowing eyes that glowed like glowing eyes that were red. And they were big. Very, very big.

And red.

Its arms were lined with missiles, and a pulsing sphere charged with some crazy kind of plasma energy protruded from its chest. King Justice was trapped beneath feet the size of eighteen-wheelers. Steel tubes ran from the robot's neck and connected to two enormous twin rockets on its back that must've allowed it to fly.

The robot looked down at me. The light in its red eyes seemed to narrow and I awaited its next move.

But the robot didn't move. Instead, it tilted its head forward slightly, and there, eighty feet above me, I saw what appeared to be a tiny human sitting atop the robot's head.

The little man looked at me and yelled something.

"WHAT?" I yelled back.

The little man leaned over the edge of the robot's head and yelled again.

"I CAN'T HEAR YOU!" I shouted. "YOU'RE TOO FAR AWAY!"

He leaned forward a little more and gave one final effort.

"Hiyam Dada Robah!!!! Noah thinkle me Dada Robah!?" I could barely hear him call down to me.

"DID YOU SAY 'DADA ROBAH'?"

The little man slumped against the edge of his control pit and banged his head on the control board. Then, what sounded like a heavy steel trapdoor slamming shut rang from high atop the robot's head, and the little man disappeared.

It didn't seem like the robot was going to move any time soon, so I tried to free King Justice. I struggled for a minute, then a distinct *THUNK, THUNK, THUNK, THUNK, THUNK, CLUNK-CLUNK, THUNK, THUNK, THUNK, THUNK, THUNK, CLUNK-CLUNK, THUNK, THUNK, THUNK, THUNK, THUNK, CLUNK-CLUNK* echoed from inside the robot's leg. I could barely hear it at first, but it grew louder and louder until it finally stopped and a door flung open in the robot's foot.

The little man stumbled out, gasping for air like a fish out of water. He leaned against the robot's foot and hung his head.

"Give me . . . give me . . . just a second . . ."

the little man huffed, trying to catch his breath. He whipped out a thick, worn notebook from his belt. *INSTALL STUPID ELEVATOR!!!!!* he wrote in large black letters, and he stuffed the notebook back into his belt.

The little man stood about four feet tall. He was completely bald and was wearing bottle-thick glasses. Above his thin lip was an even thinner mustache. His white, coffee-stained lab coat hung down to the tops of his black shoes. Suddenly the little man leaped away from the giant robot's foot. He struck an action pose and stabbed a finger at me.

"I am Dr. Robot!!!!" he screamed. "You know why they call me Dr. Robot!?!?!"

I looked at Dr. Robot, then to the eighty-foot robot at his side.

"Because . . . uh . . . you have a really big robot?"

"NO!!!! It is because I have a really big robo — oh, that's what you said, isn't it?" Dr. Robot looked at me for a moment, as if he was unsure what to do next. He scratched his head and searched for what to say, saddened that I had ruined his dramatic introduction. "Okay. I squish you now."

Dr. Robot whipped out his notebook again.

Squish him now, he wrote.

With that, he raced back into the robot's foot. *THUNK, THUNK, THUNK, THUNK, THUNK, CLUNK-CLUNK, THUNK, THUNK, THUNK, THUNK, THUNK, CLUNK-CLUNK.* There was a brief pause and a few angry words. Then the *THUNK, THUNK, THUNK, THUNK, THUNK, CLUNK-CLUNK* began again. It slowly faded away from inside the robot as Dr. Robot ran back up eighty feet of stairs.

The robot came to life again and raised his giant foot, revealing King Justice embedded in the sidewalk like a splinter of wood shoved into a fingertip. I'd need the biggest tweezers in the world to pull him out.

I grabbed his shoulder and tugged. I would've pulled again, but I suddenly saw a large shadow on the ground beneath me.

I super-jumped to the right and the robot's giant foot smashed the spot where I had just been standing. When Dr. Robot said it was time to squish me, he really meant it!

I raced in and out of the robot's enormous, stomping feet like a super-fast ant. Again and again the robot slammed down its foot in an effort to squish me under its heel.

A high-pitched feedback squeal shot out from Dr. Robot's control pit. The robot stopped moving, and Dr. Robot appeared over the edge of the robot's head again.

"STAND STILL SO I CAN SQUISH YOU!!!!"

Apparently, Dr. Robot had found a bullhorn.

The robot bent down and tried to grab me with his hand. I easily zipped out of the way. Dr. Robot peeked over the edge. "Where are all the slow superheroes!?!?!?!?" he shouted.

"What do you want?" I asked, rolling away from the robot's palm as it tried to splat me.

"I want to SQUISH you!!!!!!!" Dr. Robot cackled.

"Besides that!"

"One insidious plan at a time!!!!!!" Dr. Robot screamed back.

"Hey! Hey! What's all the racket out here?" a voice from behind me yelled. Pumpkin Pete stomped up. "You two idiots are totally disturbing my 'me' time!" Pete eyed the little Dr. Robot sitting atop the robot's head. "Who are you supposed to be?"

"Me!?!?!? ME!?!?!!?!?" Dr. Robot shrieked.

"Yeah, you," Pumpkin Pete repeated.

I pointed a thumb at the robot. "That's Dr. Robo —"

"Shut up!!!! He asked me, not you!!!! He said 'who are you?' and looked at me, not 'who is he?' and looked at you!!!!!" Dr. Robot wailed. "I am Dr. Robot!!!! You know why they call me Dr. Robot!?!?!"

Pumpkin Pete looked at Dr. Robot, then to the eighty-foot robot. He looked at Dr. Robot, then once more to the eighty-foot robot.

"Not a clue," Pete replied.

"It is because I have a really big robot!!!!" Dr. Robot clapped his hands with delight. "Okay. I squish you now."

Pumpkin Pete barely avoided the giant robot fist as it slammed into the pavement.

"Oooo!!!! Ooooo!!!! Look at Big Orange Head One!!!! He is so very slow!!!!!" Dr. Robot joyfully squealed.

"Pete!" I called out, "we've got to help King Justice!" I raced to King Justice and pulled again. "Pete? Pete?"

I turned to see Pumpkin Pete race away as fast as he could. "Pumpkin feets, don't fail me now!" he yelled as he ran into the Sidekick Super Clubhouse.

Dr. Robot guided his robot after Pete and stomped his way through the Sidekick Super Clubhouse. A second later, Pete and the Sidekicks bolted out the back door while Dr. Robot's robot kicked and smashed the Sidekick Super Clubhouse like a crazed dog shredding a newspaper.

I was about to help, when I heard a droning sound behind me. King Justice started making a motorboat noise with his lips, drool running down his chin. "Gort!" he spat, then slipped back into unconsciousness.

"No, no, no, no," Exact Change Kid moaned. "Bite-sized rubble should be placed over there. Hand- to medium-gourd–sized rubble should be collected on the other side, and *this* spot — this spot is for non-metallic, medium-gourd–sized rubble to Australian-North-Coastal-Jellyfish–sized rubble."

"Mmmp mm mmpaah mm maa!" Boy-in-the-Plastic-Bubble Boy protested.

"That wouldn't make any sense at all, now would it?" Exact Change Kid shot back. "We have to stick with size classification and just assume the density is consistent! That's been the plan the entire time!"

I'll tell you something that's dense. Exact Change Kid, that's what. Sure we needed a plan. After all, plans are a very, very good thing to have when someone in a giant robot is trying to squish you.

Just trust me on that one.

But breaking out into rubble duty to clean up the shattered remains of the Sidekick Super Clubhouse was pointless. Evil doesn't wait for you to clean your room. It's out there, now, doing . . . I don't know . . . evil and stuff! And if it does wait, then that's pretty stupid evil and if you ask me, stupid evil is even worse than smart evil because stupid evil is just totally crazy.

"Shouldn't we be going after Dr. Robot?" I asked. "He did just chase Pumpkin Pete into the city!"

"Sure. We *could*," Exact Change Kid offered. "But a little work now will make our jobs that much easier when we get back."

"King Justice is still wedged into the ground! We have to summon the rest of the League of Big Justice! Dr. Robot is running amok!" I reminded them.

"Who's Dr. Robot?"

"HE'S THE GUY CONTROLLING THE GIANT

ROBOT THAT NEARLY SQUISHED YOU!" I ranted.

"Oh! *That's* not Dr. Robot!" Boom Boy chuckled. "That's Dada Robah."

I forced myself to calm down, and said slowly and clearly, "His name . . . is Dr. Robot."

"Why do they call him Dr. Robot?" Exact Change Kid asked.

"Because . . . he has . . . A REALLY BIG RO-BOT!" So much for being calm. "And we have to stop him from destroying the city!"

"What do you guys think?" Exact Change Kid asked the rest of the Sidekicks.

"I don't know . . ." Boom Boy began, "I still think he was saying 'Dada Robah.'"

"Yeah. Definitely 'Dada Robah,'" Spice Girl agreed. "'Dr. Robot' just makes no sense. Robots don't get sick, so why would they need a doctor?"

"By that logic, why would they need a dada robah?" I snarled.

"To buy the mama robah jewelry!" Spice Girl clapped.

"Okay, now that we've settled that . . ." Exact Change Kid handed a broom to Spice Girl.

"ARE YOU NUTS!?!?" I yelled.

"I'm sorry, but we all heard it very clearly. He

said 'Hiyam Dada Robah.' You know, Speedy, a real hero knows when to admit he's wrong," Exact Change Kid lectured.

"I don't care what his name is! We have to stop him! We have to call the League of Big Justice!"

"You're right. We do . . ." Exact Change Kid began.

I let out a huge sigh, relieved I was finally getting through.

". . . right after we clean this place up." Exact Change Kid snapped his fingers. "Come on, people! This rubble won't sort itself!"

Spice Girl shifted her scent to a mixture of basil and lavender. "Helps you concentrate," she explained as the odor permeated the air. She snatched up her broom, skipped to the far corner, and started sweeping like a crazed street cleaner with a major hate-on for dirt.

Exact Change Kid handed a second broom to Boy-in-the-Plastic-Bubble Boy, which immediately fell to the ground in front of his Giant Hamster Ball of Justice. Boy-in-the-Plastic-Bubble Boy looked at the broom for a moment, then tenuously rolled forward and over it, cracking the broomstick in two.

"He can't pick it up," I huffed to Exact Change Kid.

"That's no reason for him to get out of work duty!" Exact Change Kid responded.

Exact Change Kid took a second broom and handed it to Boy-in-the-Plastic-Bubble Boy. The result was, within seconds, Boy-in-the-Plastic-Bubble Boy was rolling back and forth over two broken brooms.

I gritted my teeth and looked around for something to punch.

"Sometimes it's best to just go with the flow," Spelling Beatrice whispered into my ear as she held up a piece of rubble to make sure it wasn't larger than her hand.

"Yeah, but this flow is like a river going over a waterfall!" I replied and looked for a medium-gourd–sized piece. "Dr. Robot is on the loose! This is a waste of time!"

"You're new, Speedy," she said, suddenly sounding like a wise old patron. "You'll understand that there's a method to everything."

"Even this?"

"Even this."

I watched Earlobe Lad carry a small piece of rubble across the room. He could only carry small pieces because he had to keep one hand free to try to plug up his ears.

"Must you always drop the rubble?" he grumbled to me, sounding crabby. "Is it that difficult to just gently lay it down? Is that asking too much? Is it?"

"Sorry, I —"

Earlobe Lad stabbed a finger at me.

"Sorry," I whispered, so low even I couldn't hear what I was saying.

"Hey! Hey! I have a question!" Boom Boy yelled out. Everyone stopped and looked to him. Earlobe Lad dropped his tiny piece of rubble and folded to the floor like a collapsing building, clutching both ears with all his giant-eared strength. "What if a piece of rubble is exactly the same size as a medium gourd?"

Exact Change Kid stopped in his tracks. "What do you mean?" he asked.

"What do you mean, what do I mean? What if a piece of rubble is exactly the same size as a medium gourd?" Boom Boy repeated.

"And . . . ?" Exact Change Kid said. His tone was that of a teacher, tired of explaining the same thing to the class for the fourth time.

"What? What?" Boom Boy's face grew red.

"I'm saying, this pile is for hand- to medium-gourd–sized rubble, right?"

"Yes . . ." Exact Change Kid hissed through clenched teeth.

"And *this* spot . . . this spot is for non-metallic, medium-gourd–sized rubble to that jellyfish."

"So . . ."

"*SO*," Boom Boy continued, "if a piece of rubble is *exactly* the size of a medium gourd it can go in either pile."

"Wow. That *is* confusing," Spice Girl agreed and stopped sweeping.

"Mmmm maam pah mmmpah," Boy-in-the-Plastic-Bubble Boy added, rolling over the splintered remains of the two brooms.

"The designations are clear enough to me, Boom Boy," Exact Change Kid said. His voice grew more syrupy. He pulled out a spiral-bound notebook from his utility belt. The thick book was like a messy bowl of spaghetti with Post-it Notes — and no matter where you stabbed your fork, you were sure to hit a meatball.

This was Exact Change Kid's Master Planner of Justice. It was crammed with every note, meeting, decision, discussion, plan, advice, schedule, and take-out delivery menu Exact Change Kid had ever encountered. It was more than five hundred pages long, and that was only from the last week.

"Your observation will be duly noted," he flippantly stated, pulling the Master Planner of Justice's Super Pencil from the side clip to scribble more notes, "but I seriously doubt we'll ever encounter a piece of rubble *exactly* the same size as a medium-sized —"

Boom Boy held up his hand. Exact Change Kid went pale.

"What's he holding?" Earlobe Lad whimpered from behind a pile of debris.

What he was holding in his explosive little hand was a piece of rubble, exactly the same size as a medium-sized gourd. Exact Change Kid stared in absolute silence. He raised his Master Planner of Justice Super Pencil, then stopped. It slowly fell back to his side, only to be followed by a more enthusiastic stab into the air, which equally withered in total silence.

"Okay, people! Listen up!" Exact Change Kid finally called out, turning his back on Boom Boy and the unquestionably exactly medium-gourd–sized piece of rubble. "I'm designating an area for a new size classification!"

As Exact Change Kid roped off the new area

for exactly medium-gourd–sized pieces of rubble, I looked to Spelling Beatrice. She mouthed the word "flow" to me, which didn't help much.

"Finally . . ." Earlobe Lad moaned to Spelling Beatrice at her silent word.

Boom Boy took the exactly medium-gourd–sized piece of rubble and placed it squarely in the middle of the newly designated area; a lone piece of rock that sat like a single giant egg on an empty blanket.

Exact Change Kid watched the whole process with an odd sense of satisfaction, as if he had, with the creation of the four- by four-foot patch of ground, solved all the world's problems.

"Anything else?" he asked, puffing his chest with a sense of pride.

Spice Girl raised her hand and jumped up and down. "I have a question, too! I have a question, too!" she gushed like a little girl sitting on Santa's lap.

"Yes?" Exact Change Kid asked.

"What's a gourd?"

I wondered if Dr. Robot would still be willing to squish me.

Chapter Nine
Evil Doesn't Wait

"Mmmm maa, pah maph paa ma. Mmaaph ma phaa mam pa mmmap. Mmmma pahh mm maaa pahp maaph. Maa mmm ma mmma pammm mamm-mam pam; maaa maaa pammm? Maa maa mapp pam ma mmmm. Mmm mamm paa 'Mammmap pha pammph' ma ma ma ma!"

The thing was, it was mesmerizing. Boy-in-the-Plastic-Bubble Boy just talked and talked to me while I stacked rubble. He never stopped, never hesitated, never once took the smallest break to consider that I didn't understand a single word he was saying. He just rolled back and forth over the now toothpick-sized broom splinters as if he didn't have a care in the world.

Then I realized he should have a care. A very, very big care if you ask me.

"Hey! Hey!" I yelled and pounded my fist against Boy-in-the-Plastic-Bubble Boy's Giant Hamster Ball of Justice. "How do you go to the bathroom?"

Boy-in-the-Plastic-Bubble Boy stopped rolling over the splinters, but he didn't answer. He just rolled off into the corner, looking kinda sad, leaving behind shattered remains of two brooms and hope.

Okay, maybe just two brooms.

"Well done, everybody!" Exact Change Kid called out, sizing up the finished job. "I think we should be very proud of ourselves. When we started this project, it seemed impossible, but now, don't we all feel like the Little Engine that Could?"

"Could what?" Spice Girl asked.

"Just 'could,' Spice Girl. Just 'could.'"

"Oh . . . oh!" Spice Girl brightened. "The Little Engine that could. That *could*," she said, making finger quotes in the air. She looked at the numerous stacks of rubble divided by size and composition. Then she looked at me. "I don't get it."

"Okay, gang, let's break for the day and reconvene at o-eight-hundred hours for Sidekick roll call," Exact Change Kid said and brushed the dust from his Spandex.

"What!?" I burst out.

"For the love of Pumpkin Pete! Would someone *please* shut him up!" Earlobe Lad groaned and banged his head repeatedly against the wall.

"How can you go home now?" I continued. At this point, I didn't care if Earlobe Lad became Broken Eardrum Lad — I wasn't about to stop or be quiet for anyone.

"You're right, you're right, Speedy, and I apologize," Exact Change Kid immediately responded.

Finally! We were getting somewhere.

"Okay, who should we elect as MVS?" Exact Change Kid asked.

"MVS? What the heck is MVS?" I was afraid to hear the answer, knowing it had nothing to do with stopping Dr. Robot.

"MVS. M. V. S. Most Valuable Sidekick. It's a boomtacular honor," Boom Boy explained. "We always elect an MVS after a job well done. They get a plaque and the closest parking space to the Sidekick Super Clubhouse for a whole month!"

"But none of us drive!" I reminded him.

"Not legally, you mean." Boom Boy nudged

me with a gentle elbow to the ribs. In front of me, he dangled a pair of car keys that he had lifted from his father's pocket.

"Okay, everyone get out their secret ballots," Exact Change Kid began and pulled out a small square of paper from his utility belt. "I have extra pencils if anyone needs one."

"I do! I do!" Spice Girl enthused. "Do you have one in purple? I love purple!"

"No, sorry," Exact Change Kid noted, holding out a handful of yellow number twos.

"Oh. Oh . . ." Spice Girl slumped. She stared at the yellow pencils in Exact Change Kid's hand for a moment, then looked up. Tears welled in the corners of her eyes. "I don't feel like voting anymore," she said.

"Are all of you crazy!? Am I the only one who realizes what's going on here? While we hand out yellow pencils and ballots and sweep up trash and categorize rubble, the city is in danger! Dr. Robot is running free, doing who knows what at this very moment! We're sidekicks! This is what we've been trained to do! This is our moment to shine! We have powers! Well, some of us have powers," I corrected, noticing that Earlobe Lad was wadded up in a fetal position and trying desperately to stuff pillows in his giant ears. "We have a responsibility to fulfill! We have a duty to uphold! We are the heroes of the future, and the heroes of today need our help! And they need it NOW! So who's with me!? Huh? WHO'S WITH ME!?"

Boom Boy took the eraser on his yellow pencil and rubbed it on his secret ballot. "Well. You just lost *my* vote for MVS."

"Evil can wait until we finish our election," Spice Girl pointed out.

"No! Evil can't wait! It's not like your mom parked at the curb waiting for you to get out of school! Evil has no time-outs!" I spouted back.

"Okay, a quick vote, and then we go crush evil, okay? Would that make you happy?" Exact Change Kid offered.

"Fine!" I growled back. I folded my ballot in two and slapped it into Exact Change Kid's hand.

He collected the rest of the ballots and opened the first one. "Okay, a vote for Boom Boy."

"Boom!" Boom Boy burst out and gave a hearty thumbs-up.

"And . . . a vote for Spelling Beatrice!" Exact Change Kid read, opening the second ballot. "This might be a close one."

My foot was tapping super fast. Being able to run 102 miles per hour has odd side effects that you'd never consider. Like, I can tap my foot so fast, the rubber heel of my shoes will vibrate off. I thought it was a real cool trick until my mom started making me buy my own shoes.

"Okay, and the third vote is for . . ." Exact Change Kid opened the next ballot and stopped. "It's blank."

"Blank?" Spice Girl asked. "Is he a new member? If he is, tell him 'Blank Boy' sounds a lot better than just 'Blank.' Don't you think?"

"No, the ballot's blank."

"That's mine," I said, risking everybody flipping out because it was supposed to be secret ballot.

"Hey. Hey. How're we supposed to elect somebody if you don't vote?" Boom Boy asked.

"I didn't think it would matter. Let's just count the votes and get going!"

"'Didn't matter'?" Exact Change Kid was shocked. "Your vote always matters! You don't have to love the system, Speedy, but that's no reason to throw your vote away!"

"Fine!" I snapped and grabbed the blank ballot. I slashed a quick X in a box and thrust it back into Exact Change Kid's hand.

"Okay . . . ," Exact Change Kid said, unfolding

the ballot I had just given him as if nothing happened. "The next secret ballot is for . . ." He read my ballot silently, then took a deep breath and closed his eyes, just like my dad does when he sees I haven't mowed the lawn.

"What?" I asked.

"You can't vote for yourself." He held out the ballot to show me the X by my name. "It's just not fair play."

See, the thing is, I have super speed. I can run really, really fast. Stop for a second and think about what it would be like to run faster than most cars; to be so fast that you are already gone before people even knew you were there. I can actually create wind. Sure it's a small, zipping breeze, but it's pretty darn cool anyway.

Now imagine having all these powers and instead of using them to save the world, you're being handed a small white piece of stupid paper because you voted for the wrong stupid person in the stupid election to vote for a stupid sidekick to be the stupidest most valuable stupid sidekick who is stupid!

If I had Boom Boy's power, I'd have blown up hours ago.

I pulled the ballot from Exact Change Kid's hand and crumbled it into a ball. "Then I vote for you," I growled.

"You can't vote for me."

"Why not?"

"Because it's supposed to be a *secret* ballot and you just told everyone who you're voting for."

"He's right," Spice Girl whispered to me. "That makes it not secret."

I clawed a new ballot from Exact Change Kid's hand. My burning eyes never left his as I scratched a dark, black *X* on the ballot and pressed it back into his hand.

Exact Change Kid took my ballot and immediately unfolded it. "The next *secret* vote is for . . . Boom Boy!"

"Double Boom!" Boom Boy cheered and patted me on the back.

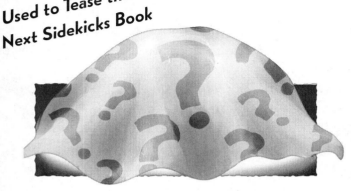

"What are they doing now?" the voice asked.

"Voting, O Great Leader," the minion replied.

"Voting?"

"Yes. Voting."

"I see."

There was a moment of silence while the voice considered the possibilities.

"Voting for what?" the voice finally asked.

"We're not sure."

"I see."

Again, silence. The voice had not seen this eventuality. There was a reason. There must be. If only the voice could crack the enigma of this event.

"Who won?" the voice finally asked.

"Boom Boy, we believe."

"I see."

Possibilities, endless possibilities unfolded like an onion smashed against a wall.

"And what happened after he won? Do we know?"

"Yes, O Great Leader. He ran to the Sidekick Super Parking Lot and moved his car to the spot closest to the Sidekick Super Clubhouse."

"Moved his — he's not old enough to drive, is he!?"

"By our records, no."

"What kind of parents allow their children to drive before they're legally able!?"

"Bad parents, O Great Leader. Bad parents."

"Of all the irresponsible things I've ever heard! When I rule the world, I'll have a thing or two to say to Boom Boy's mother and father about parenting, I'll tell you that much!"

"Will you tell them your ideas on parenting before or after you destroy Boom Boy?"

The voice thought for a moment, considering the multitude of options like a master studying a chessboard.

"After. That way I can blame it on them."

It's really not that hard to find an eighty-foot robot being driven by a four-foot madman bent on squishing everything taller than he was.

I had left the sidekicks behind to free King Justice and send the word out to the other members of the League of Big Justice. Since Dada Ro — I mean Dr. Robot — had had difficulty squishing me before, I volunteered to delay him until the others showed up.

The streets were oddly quiet. I guess when someone comes stomping through town in a giant robot, people naturally get the heck out. Luckily, I didn't see anyone seriously hurt.

I couldn't say the same for the buildings.

It looked like someone had taken a bowling ball about the size of the moon and hurled it down Main Street. The robot's giant footprints were embedded in the street and the buildings to either side were little more than rubble.

Boy, Exact Change Kid would be in heaven cleaning up this place.

I zig-zagged through the debris. The distant pounding of the robot's fists grew louder and louder as I closed ground at 85 miles per hour. I zipped around one last corner, then skidded to a stop.

". . . NO!!!!! It is because I have a really big robot!!!!" Dr. Robot clapped his hands with delight. He was shouting through his bullhorn to the driver of an ice-cream truck that had crashed into the robot's foot. "Okay. I squish you now."

"Not so fast, Dr. Robot!" I called out.

Dr. Robot and his robot both turned their heads to face me. "So!!!! You have come back to be squished again!?!?!?"

"You never squished me the first time."

"I did so!!!!"

"No, you did not!"

"Did!!!!"

"Not!"

"Did!!! Did!!! Did!!!"

"If you squished me, then why am I still here?"

Dr. Robot stopped and glared at me. He leaned over the edge of his control pit and petted the brow of his giant robot. "Don't listen to him," Dr. Robot said in a soft voice while he gently rubbed the robot. "We did so squish him."

"Why are you squishing everything?"

"Once I squish everything, no one will call me Shorty! They will look up to me and say, 'Oh, Dr. Robot! You are so tall!' And I will say, 'Yes! I am tall!' And then they'll say, 'You are so tall! You are tallest of anyone!' And then I will say, 'Because I squished you! Now you are Shorty!' And then they will say, 'Yes, Dr. Robot! You are tallest! Hey! Hey! How's the weather up there, Dr. Robot?' And I will say, 'Shut up! Shut up! Stop making fun of me for being so tall or I will unsquish you!' And then they will point and laugh and say, 'You are not Dr. Robot! You are Dr. Beanpole!' And I will say, 'Shut up! Shut up! Shut up!' And they will say, 'Dr. Beanpole! Dr. Beanpole! Dr. Beanpole!' And I will say, 'Shut up! Shut up! Shut up!'" Here, he paused for a moment. "Well, perhaps it won't go exactly like that, but I think you get my meaning!"

"I'm sorry, Dr. Robot, I just can't let you go

around and squish everything because you want to be the tallest person around."

"Oh really! And how are you going to stop me!!?!? Can you grow to eighty-one-feet tall!?!?! Do you have your own giant robot!?!?!? I don't think so!!!!" Once again Dr. Robot pulled out his notepad and furiously scribbled something inside. Most likely "Squish him now," because once he was done, he peered back over the edge and shouted, "I squish you now!"

The ice-cream man had long since run to safety, leaving me and Dr. Robot alone among the rubble. We were like two gunfighters in the Old West, staring each other down from opposite ends of the street at high noon. That is, if Old West gunfighters wore Spandex or rode around in eighty-foot robots squishing things.

This time, I made the first move. I grabbed some fallen telephone cables and quickly ran circles around the robot's legs, wrapping them tightly. With any luck, the robot wouldn't be able to walk and would tumble to the ground with its first step.

The robot lifted its foot and ripped through the cables. So much for luck.

This time, Dr. Robot meant business. The robot's hands extended at the wrists, and thick steel tendrils shot out from each arm. They squirmed at me like metallic octopus arms. A powerful electric charge shuddered through each one, sending sparks flying, and I knew that one false move and I'd be cooked blacker than my Aunt Georgia's beef brisket.

I had no protection against the attack and ran in the opposite direction. The tendrils shot after me. I cut around a pile of rubble, only to see more tendrils coming from the other side. I raced up the small rubble mountain at 62 miles per hour and jumped off the top. The tendrils collided with each other in a bright blast of electrical energy.

As the dead tendrils retracted back into the robot's wrists, I landed at the bottom of the rubble pile with a dull thud. Pain shot through my shoulder, but I didn't have a second to recover as the robot's giant foot came barreling down toward me. I rolled as fast as I could to the side and the foot landed in the exact spot where I had been with a thunderous boom. Dirt sailed into the air and debris exploded outward, tearing into my Spandex and skin.

I stumbled to my feet as the robot's fist drove

into the street next to me. The impact thrust me into the air and I smashed into the side of a ruined building.

I dove to the side as the robot's foot sailed over my head and pulverized the rest of the building.

"Stand back and let me spread the butter of justice over the nooks and crannies of evil!" a voice called out behind me.

It was King Justice! He was here with the Side-kicks! Now Dr. Robot was really going to get a pounding. But when I raced up to King Justice, he was encased in a giant block of cement.

"We couldn't get him out," Spelling Beatrice explained when she saw my face. "So we just chiseled a big hole in the pavement."

"He looks like a Twinkie!" I gasped.

And he did. Like a huge cement Twinkie with pink superhero filling. His body was still jammed into the large cement mass and his head stuck out like a broken jack-in-the-box.

"How is he going to fight like this?" I huffed.

"Prepare the Super Catapult of Justice!" King Justice cried out, as if to answer my question.

Boom Boy and Spice Girl wheeled over the huge catapult on which King Justice's block of cement was sitting.

"This time, you'll not catch King Justice napping, Dada Robah!" he yelled.

"His name is Dr. Robot," I said.

Exact Change Kid rolled his eyes. "Here we go again."

Boom Boy pushed a large red button on the catapult and King Justice and his block of cement rocketed into the air toward the giant robot.

"I shall gnaw on your metal hide with my mighty Molars of Virtue!" King Justice shouted as he hurtled toward Dr. Robot.

The massive chunk of cement hit the robot in the head, ricocheted off the side and sailed several blocks through the air.

"Have courage, my sidekicks!" King Justice yelled as he soared through the air. "I shall return! But for now, I must grit! My! Teeth! And prepare for the King of all Ouchies!"

And with that, King Justice plummeted to the earth and hit the street with the impact of a small meteor rocketing into the ground.

"You heard him, sidekicks! Let's get this robot!" I yelled out.

"Run away!" Earlobe Lad shouted and raced for safety. The others quickly followed. I should have joined them. I would have joined them, but as far as I'm concerned, no one, and I mean no one, lets King Justice ricochet off their head without me having something to say about it.

But King Justice's attempt gave me an idea. The key wasn't to fight the robot, but the man behind the robot. I *could* wait for the rest of the League of Big Justice to arrive, but I couldn't take the chance Dr. Robot would hurt more people.

I ran into a nearby building — one of the few that was still standing. The moment I raced into the lobby, the robot's massive foot kicked through the front doors. I bolted for the stairs as part of the ceiling collapsed. I raced up the staircase at 32 miles per hour. At the third floor, the robot's giant hand smashed through the wall and nearly pinned me, but I rolled under the fingers and rocketed up past the fourth and fifth floors.

At the sixth floor, the hand broke through the wall, bringing rubble crashing down. A large rock hit my shoulder. It felt dislocated. Pain shot through my body faster than Pumpkin Pete running away from danger.

But I had to continue. I had to because King Justice said, "Have courage." He said nothing about agents or insurance or tailors, or even using your powers to get a date with the cutest girl in school. And if I didn't have courage, if I didn't face this danger, what kind of hero would I be?

One unworthy of wearing the mask, that's what. One unworthy of walking in the shadow of King Justice.

I grabbed my shoulder and ran through the fingers of the robot's closing fist. I ran past the seventh, eighth, and ninth floors and finally out onto the roof.

I bolted through the door and instantly skidded to a stop.

Dr. Robot was ready. The missiles that lined the robot's arm, *all* the missiles that lined the robot's arm, were now pointed at the building.

"I am done squishing you!!!!" Dr. Robot bellowed. "Now I blow you up!!!! We shall see how fast you run when your legs are on the moon!!!!"

Dr. Robot stopped and grabbed his notebook. *Blow up Race-Around Boy so legs on moon,* he scribbled.

He hit the launch button. Fire burst from the

tail exhaust of all twelve missiles as they blasted toward the building.

There was no time to think. There was no time to be afraid. There was only time to act. I ran toward the building's edge. I ran faster than I had ever run before. My legs ached. My feet pounded. My shoulder burned. I reached the edge and jumped.

The missiles hit the building. A violent explosion rocked behind me and the booming sounds of destruction filled my ears. The shockwave and the momentum from my speed carried me toward the robot's head. I wish I could say I took aim, but I didn't. I leaped blindly, hoping I would be able to reach the robot's control pit and Dr. Robot.

I sailed through the air and prepared to land on top of Dr. Robot. It was time to deal justice. It was time to kick evil's butt, and I was just the sidekick to do it! Adrenaline pumped through my veins and I knew I was going to be a hero and save the day!

That was when the robot's hand swept through the air and swatted me like a giant, Spandex-wearing fly.

Chapter Thirteen
Swatted Like a Giant, Spandex-Wearing Fly

It's strange, the things you think when you sail through the air before you splat like a bug on a windshield.

Chapter Fourteen
Things I Thought as I Sailed Through the Air Before I Splatted Like a Bug on a Windshield

1) Prudence Cane.
2) Who's gonna feed my fish?
3) Will this hurt?
4) I hope I'm wearing clean underwear.
5) Will it still be clean after I hit the ground?
6) Do my parents *really* think Jerry Lewis is funny?
7) Why do they say *"Dial* a phone number" when you're just pushing buttons?
8) Pumpkin Pete was right about insurance.
9) Oh. Here comes the ground.
10) PrudenceCanePrudenceCanePrudence-CanePrudenceCanePrudenceCanePrud —
11) What's that?

I don't know.

I really don't.

But it came from nowhere. It came from above me, a brown blur. It flew fast, faster than anything I had ever seen and before I knew it, I was on the ground. It placed me there as gentle as a feather, then as quickly as it had swooped down on me, it shot into the sky like a human lightning bolt.

It saved my life and I didn't even know what it was.

"Thanks . . ." I stammered to the empty blue sky.

"Hurry up and die!" I heard Dr. Robot yell

from behind me. "You are putting me way behind on squishing schedule!" He took both hands and thrust out his notebook. If I had super-powered eyes, I could've seen that it said: *9:00–9:30: Squish. 9:30–10:00: Breakfast. 10:00–12:00: Squish more.*

Before I could respond, a section of the robot's chest plate opened up, revealing a second arsenal of smaller missiles. The moment the chest plate locked into position, a missile fired. I zipped quickly to one side and the missile zoomed by . . . then made a sharp, arcing turn.

Heat seekers!

I raced away, but the missile zeroed in and was hot on my tail. I can outrun a car, but a missile!? I had seconds, maybe less. I bolted around a street corner and spotted a burning car that had been squished by Dr. Robot. It was my only chance.

The missile shot around the corner as I ran behind the flames. The missile locked onto the hotter heat source as I hurried to safety.

Impact! The explosion sent me somersaulting down the street like a tumbleweed. I gave a sharp yelp as I landed on my wounded shoulder. But there would be no rest, not yet.

Not when I finally had a plan.

Well, I guess my others were plans, too, but this one might actually be good. And when you're fighting a giant robot bent on squishing you, that single word "good" can be the difference between success and street pancake.

Across the street was a hardware store. I raced in at 50 miles per hour and raced out at 65 with a can of kerosene. I ran back to the giant robot.

"I make you a deal, Race-Around Boy!" Dr. Robot shouted down to me through his bullhorn. "Let me squish you and I promise I will only squish you very little!!!!!"

"Why would I want to do that?"

Dr. Robot was frustrated I didn't see the generosity of his offer. "Then you will be second tallest once I squish everything!!!! They will look up to you and say, 'Oh, Race-Around Boy, you are so very tall!' And you will say, 'Yes, I am tall.' And then they'll say, 'You are so tall! You are second tallest of anyone!' And then you will say, 'Because Dr. Robot squished you! Now you are Shorty!' And then they will say, 'Hey! Hey! How's the weather up there, Race-Around Boy?' and I will say, 'Don't listen to them, that is just Shorty joke they say.' And they will say, 'We bet it is cold up there, but not as cold as Dr. Robot! He is tall like beanpole!' And I will say, 'Shut up! Shut up! Stop making fun of me for being so tall or I will unsquish you!' And then they will point and laugh and say, 'You are not Dr. Robot! You are Dr. Beanpole!' And I will say, 'Shut up! Shut up! Shut up!' And they will say, 'Dr. Beanpole! Dr. Beanpole! Dr. Beanpole!' And I will say, 'Shut up! Shut up! Shut up!'"

Here, he paused for a moment. "Well, perhaps it won't go exactly like that . . ."

While Dr. Robot ranted, I poured the kerosene on the robot's foot and raced down the street to the burning wreckage where the first missile had hit.

"I'll take that as a 'no'!" Dr. Robot called after me and fired another heat seeker.

I grabbed a chunk of burning debris and zoomed around the corner. I was hoping the missile would lock onto the larger burning wreck like the old one did, but no luck; it chased after me.

It was going to be close. I raced back around the block, knowing that the missile would have to take wide turns, and ran as fast as I could back to Dr. Robot. At the last moment, I threw the small piece of the burning wreck I had been carrying at the robot's feet and the kerosene burst into flames.

"Hahaha!!!! You cannot burn down robot!!!!" Dr. Robot laughed through the bullhorn. "That is why I stopped making them out of wood!!!! I think your brain already squished!!!! You are stupidest one of all!!!! I laugh at — uh-oh."

The heat-seeking missile rocketed around the corner. It locked onto the larger heat source: the flames on the robot. The missile blasted into its foot, blowing up the leg from the knee down. The robot teetered. Dr. Robot struggled at the controls to keep it upright, with no luck. The robot toppled like an enormous redwood felled to the ground.

"Quick!!!!" Dr. Robot yelled. "Run under robot so I can squish youuuuuuuuuuuu!"

Needless to say, I did no such thing.

"Pumpkin Powers, activate!" Pumpkin Pete yelled, climbing out of a nearby sewer hole. He raced up to the felled robot and leapt onto its face. "Stand back, kid, and let a real superhero take over!"

As soon as Pete made his announcement, the news crews seemed to appear from thin air. Microphones and cameras huddled around the triumphant Pumpkin Pete.

"Pumpkin Pete! Pumpkin Pete!" one newsperson called out. "How'd you defeat the robot!?"

I turned to leave. I knew Pete didn't like sharing . . . anything.

"I didn't do it alone!" Pete answered. I stopped in my tracks. "I had the help of a little friend . . ."

Could it be . . . was he actually going to give me some credit?

". . . A little friend called Pow Soda!" Pete popped open a can of Pow and took a big gulp. "End the crime spree of thirst with Pow Soda: The Soft Drink of Superheroes."

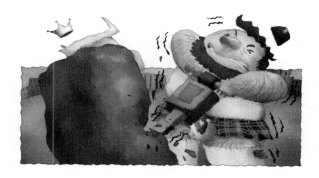

The jackhammer pounded into the side of the cement. Bits and shards flew off and hit Captain Haggis in the body and face. The rest of the League of Big Justice had arrived just in time . . . just in time to sign autographs and get King Justice out of the cement block.

"Ack!" Captain Haggis grumbled and spat out a small chunk of cement. "Next tyme ge'yesself stuck in s'm jelly!"

"Head! Pounding! Senses assaulted by the mad mallet of destruction! Must! Have! Aspirin! Oh! Whatta headache!" King Justice grimaced as Captain Haggis took a break from chiseling at the cement that still encased his body.

I dropped two aspirin on King Justice's tongue and poured a glass of water into his mouth.

"Ah! Relief! On its way!" King Justice rejoiced.

Dr. Robot had been taken into custody. His giant robot still lay strewn across the city streets, wires sparking as the final electric life drained from its body.

The medics had put my arm in a sling. My shoulder was slightly separated, which was fine with me. I could just see Prudence Cane's face now as I recounted my heroics and showed her my wounds while on our date.

"Sigh," she will say and bat her eyes at me. "Siiiigh."

"Yes," I will reply. "Siiiiigh."

"You are so brave," she will say. "Siiiiiiigh."

"Yes, I am so brave," I will reply. "I could not let Dr. Robot get to your house. My life meant nothing, if it would have stopped him."

"Siiiiiiiigh," she will say and bat her eyes even more at me.

"Yes," I will reply. "Siiiiigh."

I. Can't. Wait!

I had to go meet Miles and stuff the contest box with Prudence's name. I still wasn't proud of the whole idea, but I sure was excited about it, and sometimes excitement just seemed to kick pride's butt.

But there was one last thing I had to do before I raced off to set my own plan into motion . . .

"Are there any new members of the League of Big Justice?" I asked.

"None," King Justice replied.

"Any new superheroes in town?"

King Justice shook his head.

"It's just that, I swear I was saved by someone; someone who shot across the sky like a brown lightning bolt."

King Justice perked up. "What!? A *brown* . . . Impossible!"

"I swear! It came from nowhere and saved me!"

King Justice looked at me, as if he was probing me for a deeper truth. "I . . . I must go . . ."

King Justice hopped like he was in a potato-sack race and managed to bounce his cement block to the Super Catapult of Justice. "Launch me!" he cried out to anyone who would listen.

"With pleasure," Pumpkin Pete replied and hit the launch button.

"King Justice! King Justice!" I called after

him as he was flung into the sky, "What was it!? What!?" It was too late. Whatever secret he may have had about a brown lightning bolt he took with him into the sky.

With the mystery fresh in my head and Prudence Cane waiting, I only hoped that once King Justice did land, it wasn't on someone's house.

Chapter Seventeen
The Winner

The funny thing was, the box with all the contest names was under my direct supervision the whole time. That's what really irks me. I just don't get it. I really don't.

Miles had come up with a great idea: let the school principal, Mr. Withers, pull the "random" name from the box and announce the winner. That way, there would be no suspicion we had rigged the contest by stuffing the box with Prudence's name.

And the box was with me the whole time. The *whole* time.

So imagine me, in my Speedy costume, standing on the stage at my school with Mr. Withers and Miles. Students, mostly girls, were packed in front of us like sardines, each one eagerly hoping their name would be called, and most of them hoping they could choose Charisma Kid instead of me.

The tension was killing everyone but me. I gave Miles a wink — a wink of confidence, a wink that said, *Hello Prudence, my name is Speedy.* A wink that said SUCCESS!

Miles handed Mr. Withers the box. He covered his eyes with one hand and stabbed his other into the mass of awaiting *Prudence Cane*s. After a few seconds of stirring, he pulled his hand from the box, a single piece of folded paper clenched between his thumb and index finger.

Mr. Withers handed the piece of paper to Miles. Miles stepped before the microphone and unfolded the small piece of white paper.

"And the winner is . . ." Miles stopped. He looked at the paper for a moment, then to me.

"Read it . . ." I whispered without moving my lips.

"The . . . uh . . . winner is . . ."

Miles stopped again. I grabbed the microphone, playing along with his tension-building drama.

"Hurry up, Miles!" I said through the microphone, play-acting. "The pressure is killing me!"

"Okay," Miles sighed. "The winner is . . ."

I walked down the street by myself in my Speedy costume. The newsstand across the street from the movie theater had stacks of newspapers, all with the headline PUMPKIN PETE STOPS DADA ROBAH! CITY SAVED!

"Can you believe it?" the newsstand vendor said to me. "If it weren't for Pumpkin Pete, Dada Robah would've squished us all."

"His name is 'Dr. Robot,'" I corrected.

"Whose?" the vendor questioned.

"Who!? The guy with the giant robot, that's who!"

"Dr. Robot! That doesn't make any sense at all," a man at the newsstand said.

"Who's Dr. Robot?" a woman asked.

"The guy who built and rode around in the giant robot trying to squish everyone!" I explained in an irritated tone.

"Oh!" the lady said, "You mean Dada Robah."

"No! I mean Dr. Robot! Dr.RobotDr.Robot-Dr.Robot!"

The man, the woman, and the newsstand

vendor all looked at me for a moment, slightly confused.

"Isn't it a little early for Halloween?" the man finally asked.

I shook my head and walked across the street to the movie theater. I pulled some money from my utility belt and bought a ticket.

"Isn't it a little early for Halloween?" the girl at the box office asked.

I grabbed my ticket and marched into the building.

The moment I walked through the double doors of the theater, a hand stabbed into the air and waved to me. I trudged down the aisle and plopped into the empty seat.

"This is easily the greatest day of my life! I can't believe I won! I am so thrilled to meet you. When Mr. Withers pulled my name from the box, I nearly died! I just . . . I just . . . I don't even know what to say!"

And so the principal had pulled the name out of the box. Miles had read it. The winner had jumped up and down in the crowd of students packed before the stage and, although he would never realize it, Jerry Stone finally got to sit in the seat I was so hopefully reserving for Prudence Cane.

"Shut up," I groaned, "and give me some popcorn."

As I silently begged for the relief of darkness with the start of the movie, Jerry Stone began his "adventurous" stories about every single superhero he had created for his own comic book series and showed me all the pages he had drawn himself.

Somewhere, somehow, I knew that Charisma Kid was responsible; responsible and laughing until he cried.

"And the winner is . . ."

The air was so thick with tension, you could cut it with a knife, if tense air could be cut.

"The winner is . . . Spice Girl!" Exact Change Kid read from the paper he had pulled from the box.

"Yay!!!!" Spice Girl squealed and jumped from her chair.

"Lemme see that box!" Boom Boy roared.

"No!" Exact Change Kid clenched the box tightly in both hands.

"Mam pam pam mam maaam pam!" Boy-in-the-Plastic-Bubble Boy angrily accused.

"What!? I'd never do that!" Exact Change Kid responded and clutched the box even tighter.

"Get him!!!" Earlobe Lad whispered and tackled Exact Change Kid.

The box flew from his hands. Boom Boy ran over and tore off the lid. He grabbed a handful of the folded pieces of paper that were stuck inside.

"Look!" Boom Boy called out, unfolding several of the contest entry pieces. "They *all* say Spice Girl!"

"Hurray!" yelled Spice Girl. "I win everything!"

Earlobe Lad, Boom Boy, Spelling Beatrice, and Boy-in-the-Plastic-Bubble Boy all left the Sidekick Super Clubhouse Room of Meetingness in disgust, leaving Exact Change Kid in a pile of scrap paper pieces that all read SPICE GIRL.

"Hooray for me!" Spice Girl cheered. "What'd I win!? What'd I win!?" She jumped up and down like a pogo stick.

"You win a date with me," Exact Change Kid said, looking up from the pile of paper.

"Oh," Spice Girl replied. "I'm sad now."

Author Bios
Biographies of the Authors!

Dan Danko attributes his love of comic books to his childhood belief that he's from another planet. To this day, he has yet to be proven wrong.

Dan lists one of his greatest accomplishments as being fluent enough in Japanese to speak to a dim-witted seven-year-old. If Dan isn't watching Lakers' games, you'll find him traveling to any country that has a traveler's advisory from the U.S. State Department — much to his mother's dismay.

He's the tall one.

Tom Mason's love of comic books and all things superhero-ey began when he had the flu and his parents bought him a stack of comics and sent him to the doctor.

When he's not selling his family's heirlooms on eBay or scuba diving off the California coast, he enjoys playing horseshoes with a long list of celebrities, all of whom once appeared on *The Love Boat.*

He's the cute one.

Dan and **Tom** are former editors and writers for Malibu and Marvel Comics, and they have also written for the TV series *Malcolm in the Middle* and *Rugrats*. They've been story editors on *Pet Alien* and on Nickelodeon's *Brothers Flub*.

Their combined height is twelve feet, one inch.

P.S. And they still read comic books!